Dear Parents/Caregivers:

Children learn to read in stages, and all children develop reading skills at different ages. **Fisher-Price® Ready Reader Storybooks™** were created to encourage children's interest in reading and to increase their reading skills. The stories in this series were written to specific grade levels to serve the needs of children from preschool through third grade. Of course, every child is different, so we hope that you will allow your child to explore the stories at his or her own pace.

All of the stories in this series are fun, easy-to-follow tales that have engaging full-color artwork. Children can move from books that have the simplest vocabulary and concepts, to each progressive level to expand their reading skills. With the **Fisher-Price® Ready Reader Storybooks™**, reading will become an exciting adventure for your child. Soon your child will not only be ready to read, but will be eager to do so.

Educational Consultants: Mary McLean-Hely, M.A. in Education: Design and Evaluation of Educational Programs, Stanford University; Wendy Gelsanliter, M.S. in Early Childhood Education, Bank Street College of Education; Nancy A. Dearborn, B.S. in Education, University of Wisconsin-Whitewater

Fisher-Price® Ready Reader Storybook™
Sara's Secret Hiding Place

SARA ONLY

Written by C. Louise March • Illustrated by Art Mawhinney

Modern Publishing
A Division of Unisystems, Inc.
New York, New York 10022

Sara has three brothers.

Sara likes to play alone in
her tree house.

Dan misses Sara.

"Sara, can I come up?"
Dan asks.

"No," Sara says. "I'm fighting a dragon."

"I can fight a dragon,"
Dan says.

Sara and Dan fight the dragon.

Mike misses Sara.

"Sara, can I come up?"
Mike asks.

"No," Sara says. "We're playing pirates."

"I can be a pirate,"
Mike says.

They find buried treasure.

"Where's Sara?" her mom asks.

"In her tree house" Keith says.

Keith misses Sara.

"Sara, can I come up?"
he asks.

"No," Sara says.
"We are digging."

"I can dig, too," Keith says.

They dig up dinosaur bones.

"Can we come back?"
Mike asks. "We can play
cowboys!" Sara nods.

Sara likes playing with
her brothers after all.